JETT THE SPY

THE SECRET TO FINDING TRUE FRIENDS

MIA KELLY

AND

EMMA BONARDI

Published June 2021

ANEWPRESS

DEDICATION

We dedicate this book to the good friends who have shown us an endless amount of support and kindness through all of our challenges in life.

The day finally came. Jett had been waiting all of his life, but at last he turned eight years old! This may not seem like such a big deal to normal kids, but Jett's life is a little out of the ordinary. Jett was born into a family of spies and turning eight means he gets to be enrolled at the Top-Secret Academy for Spies in Training- Spy School, as they call it.

His parents graduated from this school and are now elite spies, so he wants to be just like them when he grows up. This school is essential for every spy to learn basic skills and to train for the job. Tomorrow, he takes the bus to Snoopsville to start his training and receive his first mission!

Before the bus arrived at his house the next day, Jett's parents pulled him over to talk. "We want to share our secrets on how to be a successful spy," his mom said. "Being a spy is all about being clever and blending in. You have to find out who your allies are, and always stick to the mission. Follow this advice and we're sure you'll be a great spy in no time!" his dad told him. As the bus pulled up, they gave him a hug and shouted, "We believe in you, Jett!" And he waved back.

SPY SCHOOL

After a while, the bus finally reached Spy School. Jett introduced himself to his fellow classmates and took a seat for his first lesson. After learning the basics to spying, it was time to receive his first assignment. The first mission each student is sent on is to study a basic topic, and Jett was nervous to hear his. "Jett! You will be going to Winchester Elementary School undercover as a new student.

8

Your job is to find out the difference between friends you can trust and those you can't!" He was excited; it is very important for a spy to know who he can count on. With his goal in mind, Jett set out for this new school. As he left, the teacher called out to the students, "Remember that this is a top-secret academy, so if you blow your cover, there will be consequences! Also, remember that reports on your first missions are due three days from today!"

WINCHESTER ELEMENTARY SCHOOL

Before he knew it, Jett was walking up to the elementary school where his mission would take place. It was a strange building, like nothing he'd ever seen before. It was made completely out of glass and looked very futuristic. The large size of the school scared him a little, but he walked into the classroom with confidence in his new spying skills.

10

"Good morning class!" said his new teacher, Ms. Bigsby. "Today we have a new student visiting our class. Jett, please come to the front!" Jett cautiously made his way over and awkwardly smiled at the class. He was nervous because the more he talked, the easier it was for him to blow his cover and get revealed as a spy. "Jett will be sitting between Ivy and Quinton," Ms. Bigsby finished. He sat down in an empty seat next to a young boy who appeared very shy but friendly, and a girl who seemed popular and a bit bossy.

Soon after, it was time for lunch, and Jett followed his classmates to the cafeteria. He picked up his lunch of apple juice and a baloney sandwich and sat down at an empty table. Jett began to observe the kids in the class- an important part of spying is watching other people. You can learn a lot about someone by watching how they interact with others. His eye was drawn to Quinton, the boy whom he sat next to in class. He wasn't sitting with a lot of other kids, but they were all smiling. He seemed nice and made his friends laugh. Jett then looked over at Ivy's table, which

was crowded with people. Ivy was sitting in the middle, whispering to another girl, and pointing at Quinton. It was clear that she led the group and bossed everyone around. No one at her table was smiling, and Jett could tell that they all looked unhappy. He wondered what was so special about Ivy to make them still sit with her. Jett followed Ivy's pointed finger to Quinton's table and noticed how Quinton's smile faded. Jett had always been observant, and this trait is what made him want to be a spy. Even the smallest details, like the way Quinton got nervous when he noticed Ivy laughing, are very important when it comes to a mission.

After lunch, Ms. Bigsby assigned all of the students to do a relay race activity. Jett sat on the side and watched, to make sure he kept his cover. The class was split into two teams with Ivy as one team captain and Quinton as the other. The class headed outside to the field, and Ms. Bigsby gave them instructions. "One person will run to the other end of the field and once they get back, they have to high-five the next person before they start running. Got it?" The class nodded and lined up behind the cones. "On your marks, get set, go," called Ms. Bigsby, and Quinton and Ivy started running. As soon as Quinton got back to the starting line, his cheering friends high-fived him and took the lead.

Ivy was a fast runner, but when she got back to the starting line, her friends were all arguing about who got to go next. Their whole team was yelling at each other, including Ivy, and they weren't able to make a compromise. Before long, Quinton's team had finished and were celebrating. Everyone on Ivy's team was left in a bad mood and started trash-talking Quinton and his team. Jett was beginning to notice how the success of a team depends on how well they cooperate and are supportive of one another. When it comes to group missions, you don't want to be stuck with a team that doesn't have your back.

At the end of the day, Jett took the bus back to Spy School where he would be spending the night while on his mission. As he settled into bed, Jett thought about the information he had gathered during his first day at Winchester School and began his report.

With his thoughts organized, Jett fell asleep, prepared for another day as an undercover spy.

Day 1 Findings:

- Sometimes it is better to have a few good friends than a lot of friends who don't really care about you.

- Talking negatively about someone else hurts them, and words matter

- A group is more likely to succeed if you have good teamwork

The next morning, Jett arrived at Winchester bright and early. "Good morning Jett! Just the person I wanted to see," said Ms. Bigsby. "I think it's time you prepared a presentation for the class about yourself. This way, the kids will get to know you better and you can hopefully make some friends!" Jett nodded, but on the inside, he was not excited to have to share personal information with the class. Of course, no one knew he was a spy gathering information, even Ms. Bigsby, and it would be much harder now to keep his cover.

18

He didn't want to risk the consequences that Spy School would punish him with if his classmates found out the truth. "Great! Will you be ready in two days?" Ms. Bigsby asked. Jett said yes, and she walked away. He was going to have to be very careful with what he chooses to share, and he doesn't have much time to figure it out!

When class started, Ms. Bigsby took the kids outside and told them they were going to play a fun game called Wingerball. She picked the same two team captains, Ivy and Quinton. Before long, the teams were almost filled. Ivy's team had all of her friends, and so did Quinton's. Jett was the last person left, so Ms. Bigsby told him to choose whose team he wanted to be on. Jett looked over to Ivy's team. They were glaring and as soon as she saw him look over, she declared that her team was full. Jett then walked over to Quinton, and even though he had no choice but to be on his team, Quinton still smiled and welcomed him.

He turned to Jett and said, "The more the merrier!" All of his teammates gave him a high-five. Soon after, they started to play, and Jett had a blast throwing around the ball! His team easily won due to their teamwork and passing skills, and Quinton was the highest scorer! Ivy's team, on the other hand, was hogging the ball and yelling at each other, making cooperation very hard. In the end, they were sore losers, blaming their loss on Jett and Quinton's team and claimed they cheated. Jett was really glad he chose to be on Quinton's team!

The day of Jett's presentation finally came, and he was really nervous to share personal information with the class. He had never liked being the center of attention, which is one of the main reasons he became a spy; they are always working behind the scenes. At the beginning of class, Ms. Bigsby told Jett to come forward and begin his presentation. She asked, "Are you ready, Jett?" He nodded, and slowly walked to the front of the class. Now Jett was really starting to get anxious because not only was he worried about revealing his identity, but he had stage fright.

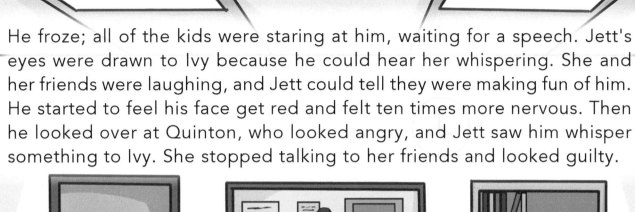

He froze; all of the kids were staring at him, waiting for a speech. Jett's eyes were drawn to Ivy because he could hear her whispering. She and her friends were laughing, and Jett could tell they were making fun of him. He started to feel his face get red and felt ten times more nervous. Then he looked over at Quinton, who looked angry, and Jett saw him whisper something to Ivy. She stopped talking to her friends and looked guilty.

Quinton smiled and gave Jett a thumbs up. Jett immediately felt more confident and supported, and he was ready to present.

Jett started to talk: "Good morning. My name is Jett Bonnelly, and I am eight years old. I am visiting from a town a couple hours away and am excited to be here at Winchester! Some of my hobbies are playing tennis, reading mystery books, and going on adventures. I look forward to getting to know all of you!" Jett's classmates gave a small round of applause, and he walked back to his seat. Quinton gave him a high five, and even Ivy flashed a smile. "Thank you, Jett," Ms. Bigsby said.

Once it was time for recess, Jett walked outside with Quinton. "I just wanted to say thanks for standing up for me back there," Jett told him. "Of course," Quinton said, and the two started to become friends. Jett felt like he could really trust Quinton because he was there for him when needed. This was the reassurance Jett needed that he was on the right track with his report.

At last, Jett's mission was over. He headed back to Spy School after saying goodbye to his classmates at Winchester and made the finishing touches to his report. He was excited to get back home to his parents and share with his fellow spies in training. Jett had learned so much about what it takes to be a true friend, and he was finally ready to venture into the world as a spy with knowledge of who he can and cannot trust-information that is essential to the success of a spy's mission!

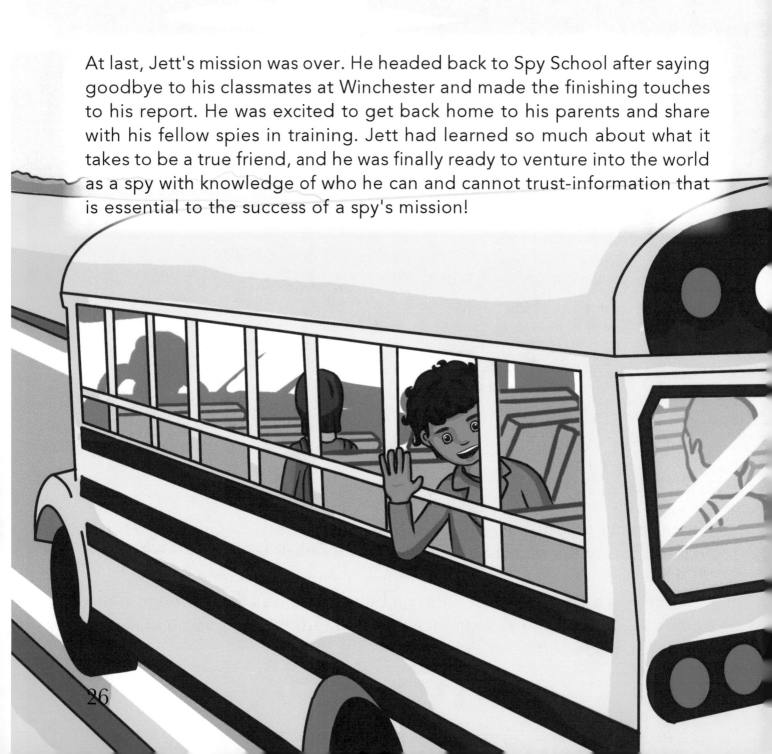

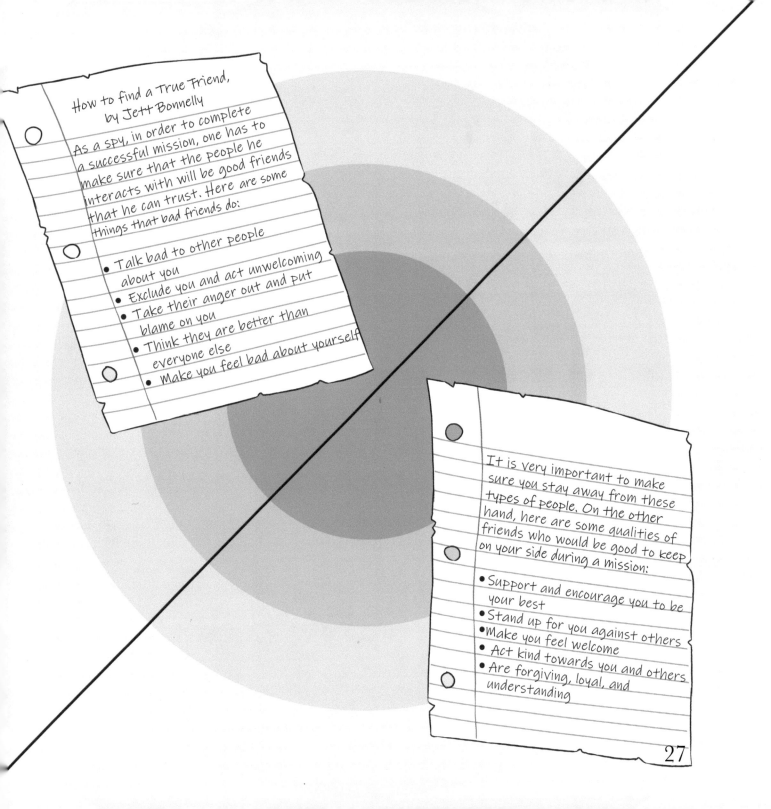

How to find a True Friend,
by Jett Bonnelly

As a spy, in order to complete a successful mission, one has to make sure that the people he interacts with will be good friends that he can trust. Here are some things that bad friends do:

- Talk bad to other people about you
- Exclude you and act unwelcoming
- Take their anger out and put blame on you
- Think they are better than everyone else
- Make you feel bad about yourself

It is very important to make sure you stay away from these types of people. On the other hand, here are some qualities of friends who would be good to keep on your side during a mission:

- Support and encourage you to be your best
- Stand up for you against others
- Make you feel welcome
- Act kind towards you and others
- Are forgiving, loyal, and understanding

27

ABOUT THE AUTHORS

Mia Kelly and Emma Bonardi are both seventeen-year-old high school students who live in the California Bay Area. Growing up best friends, they have had to navigate through many different situations where good and bad friends were involved. They have learned a lot through their experiences and feel as though this message needs to be shared with young kids so that they can learn to be better friends in the future!

Mia and Emma, Age 7

Mia and Emma, Age 17

CPSIA information can be obtained
at www.ICGtesting.com
Printed in the USA
LVHW070310280721
693914LV00001B/52